My rocking horse fell on its side

My tea table was vaporized

My dolls crumbled and fell as well

My swing set ripped in twain

My boyish dusty hair danced in the wind

My ever blue eyes stared at the sky

I am cursed; it was seven hundred and

seventy-eight.

I am *Sabbath*, as I was born on *seven hundred*

and seventy-seven. I am now seven years old; this

makes it my lucky year... if it had not been for *seven*

hundred and seventy-eight.

To make sense of my life, we must first start

with the story of my parents and for that we need to

follow my father back to a time when it was only

seven hundred and forty-four.

PART 1 – THE WORLD WE LIVED IN

The world had ended; its beauty vanished, its

life nearly extinguished overnight. When the first

five atomic bombs fell on London, what was left of the country as well as its allies had to reply with bombs of their own. Like a gigantic house of cards whose nasty wind created an avalanche of catastrophic proportion or a series of dominoes falling due to all but a light tap, the world had ended in mere hours.

By the dawn, in itself still fresh and innocent, Moscow had felt over *seventeen;* Russia itself had to wake up witnessing *seventy-four* altogether, France and Germany each received *eight,* quite a lot for a country their size. As expected, the United States received the most with *a hundred and twenty-four,* but still dim in comparison to the *three-hundred and twelve* that fell in the combined *North* and *South America.* None were spared, from Africa to Australia; any surface known to man, for reasons we will never know, less we have time to care for but a trivial matter now, had been hit. Even the oceans had their fair share of explosions, probably due to radical beliefs of the common carp, no doubt.

Much later, when my father turned the dial on a working radio, the current tally was that, for those who still cared, *seven hundred and forty-four* nuclear bombs had fallen on the earth. War was going on where war was still worth fighting; missiles still flew in the air as, I guess, Man is still stupid enough to continue its destruction instead of stepping back and looking at what it has done.

Somehow, through purpose rather than strength, my father had survived the onslaught. He tells me that before *one* fell down, he had moved to a rural piece of land on a complete whim. Only now can we look back and wonder if it was merely a whim or a divine intervention. My father has no muscles, no body fat, no mustache and no mean-looking face; he has no traits of an action hero. Little did he know, I think, that these traits might have given him an edge in the beginning of this new age. He ate so little, not by choice but just because he was never really that hungry to begin with, that the provisions

he had bought would last him for days, no, weeks.

Like millions, yet billions of his kin, he had no clue

what to do; the events were simply not sinking in.

Deciding to wait for others, my father went back in

his apartment, barricaded any entries with what little

he had at home and set his goal to only venture out

in what was now the wild once his provisions were

nearly exhausted.

Day and night, he would listen to his radio. The sources were either pre-war genuine broadcasters or simply people who had now decided to hijack airwaves; regardless, any information was relevant and although not a source of comfort, it was a *cradle of sanity*. Left to themselves, Man can become a savage beast. Without law, honor or ethics to bind them, they are free to do as they please; they are free to uphold their virtues or fall into their vices. I may be only seven, but I have seen those vices aplenty. Days on end, he would listen for the world's next move for that next move would

dictate his, but the world did not budge. *Nothing*

happened. The rare new bombs would fall but after

this count, why should they be acknowledged as

anything?

The day my father opened the door was the

day I started loving my father. Even though I was not

born yet, I can say truly in my heart that this is the

moment that my father was brought to life within

me. He acknowledged the world; the world had

changed. He smiled at the world; the world was ready to be fought. When he first told me he smiled, I had to ask why he did so; was a world in ruin worth smiling for?

"A world destroyed is a world in need to be rebuilt."

It was as if my father branded the entire world or rather the *circumstances* of the world as his own personal enemy; instead of crying at the situation, of bursting in a fit of rage or simply going

mad, he smiled. He smiled because I think he finally

knew what to do, because there was so much to be

done. You would be fair in your assumption that

smiling while staring at a destroyed world could be

considered as a type of *madness*, but he was not

mad, he was in control, he was *strong*. He says he

felt this spirit descend upon him, renewing his

energy, making him believe that his journey would

now truly start.   He tells me that he felt so

empowered *(I still laugh when he tells me that part)*

that the first thing he did was notice a gigantic man

robbing an elderly couple who had no choice but to

venture the streets. He walked to the man and

swiped whatever he had stolen and gave it back to

the couple. The giant was obviously stunned; no one

had ever tried that before so he did not know what

to do. My father had enough time to receive tearful

thanks from the old couple before he was lightly

tapped on the shoulder by the giant. He turned

around and, he tells me, that the look he had on his

face, this feeling of certainty, confidence and

strength scared the giant away. The large man

backed away, said a few foul words that father said

best not to learn, added that he did not have time

for this and walked away. Obviously, even though

my father was now *strong*, he started shaking. It was

as if the moment was now gone; his legs trembled

and his eyes opened wide as his mind replayed to

him what he had just accomplished.

"I surrender to your will," he said. *"Whatever*

must be done next, I will do."

To tell you the truth, he did not do that much

more yet and time did flow by. He did go outside; he

did find provisions that kept him going for much

longer than what a normal man would normally

need. Although he had always been thin, he tells me

that this was not the same; he said the feeling was

different, as if he simply did not need more. It was a

good thing, because plenty of people were hungry,

but that was about to change and no, not for the

best.

I know, I know, my story is rather dark is it not?

I have seen too many dark days in the short amount

of time I have been alive but my father says that,

shrouded in darkness, it is easier to spot the light,

faint as it may be. The words I have learned in my

seven years will still be of use to me when I am

seventy-seven.

I said it was about to change and it sadly did.

It turns out that war was indeed still raging on and

my father was not in a region that currently had the

upper hand. He woke up hearing a mix of cries,

shouting and gunshots. He always pauses here when

he tells me that part. He says it is truly horrible, but

when he thinks about those few seconds that he had

to listen to, that he felt as if they encompassed the

entire plight of the human race. The cries he heard

here must have been the same cries of a family in

Africa; the shouting and gunshots exchanged were

probably happening here at the same time as they

were happening in Canada. *War is a destroyer but*

strangely, a spiritual unifier.

Fists pounded on his door. He took a deep

breath. Words were shouted in a language he

understood but did not reply to.

BAM!

BAM!

BAM!

The fists were mad; the door would not last, it was

never meant to last. Father sat down on his only

chair. He smiled. He smiled when they burst in. He

smiled when they threw him on the floor, restrained

him and blinded him with a potato sack over his

head. He smiled when he was violently dumped in a

truck next to a choir of crying men, women and

children. *"It's okay,"* he calmly said to the crying

woman next to him. He felt it. He felt her as she

placed her head on his shoulder; he gently rested his

head on hers and they fell asleep.

They woke up when the truck came to a halt.

Although it was not his first day in this new world, he

tells me that waking up only to hear the same cries

he heard before was his first realization that, no, it

was no dream. Although he could not see, he heard

people being taken away from the truck. The lady

next to him fought and shrieked as someone grabbed

her.

"I'll save you," he whispered to her as if my

father could actually save anyone.

Well, why her? Throw a stick in the air and it will

definitely land on someone in need of help, in need

of being saved. Regardless, that is what happened

and the lady spoke no more. As they took him and

dragged him, he chuckled as he realized the passion

of his promise. Here he was dragged into a camp or

a prison, unknowing if it would be the last of him and

here he had been, promising freedom to a woman he

did not even have time to see.

"But I could see her."

He was thrown on the barren, hard ground

and his veil was taken off his head by another

prisoner. They stood in what was once a large

farmland whose productive soil produced no more;

towering fences covered the land where only a

handful of wooden structures, hastily erected, stood.

The men and women had not even been separated;

it was a prison still in its infant days, as if the captors

still had much to learn on how to properly imprison

someone. Slowly, almost mechanically he surveyed

the land, looking for the lady he never truly saw.

Definitely, no one had been here for ages and as

such, the prison was livelier than you could expect;

their spirit had not been shattered yet. Men

regrouped, plotted; women would tend to their

children but all that energy was brought to naught

when gunshots were heard.

Father walked around. To the first woman to come beg to him, he gave all the change he had in his pocket; that is what she wanted, probably still oblivious to the fact that it was not really worth anything anymore. To the second man he met shouting cries of rally, he nodded. The third man, well the third man was armed, so he stopped. In front of him were a few soldiers blocking his way, probably the same soldiers that brought him in in the first place? They made way to a clearly deranged and dangerous general who carried on his shoulder a

decidedly awake but calm woman. He was so big

and she was so small.

"This is your mother," father said to me.

My father inquired about the woman to the

soldier who at first laughed at the sight of a prisoner

talking in such a casual manner but, in the end, was

not as mean as he could have been. She was not in

as much trouble as it seemed to appear. The guard

calmly explained to him that soon men, women and children would be contained in barracks, cuffed without the ability to walk. Mother apparently was the first person to kick the giant general in an area that I am told generals should not be kicked in and as such was granted the first shackles.

It seems like a strange reason, it must have been a pretty awesome kick, don't you think? Father inquired a little more about the details but that was a bit too much. The soldier gave him the evil eyes;

eyes that meant that they should have struck him but did not feel like it. The barrack where mother was to be held had only a single door and no window; a single guard stood, one guard too many.

Night fell and families bundled together for heat. Some men still walked around; some still look for a way to escape, but father, father was not looking for an escape just yet. He circled mother's barrack once, twice and stopped when the guard swung his weapon his way. Truly there were no other ways to enter the barrack aside from the door,

unless, well, that was unless he crafted his own

entrance. The barrack was near the limits of the

compound blocked by a tall mountain that made

digging your way out totally impossible and as such,

it was a region that did not need much patrolling.

This, however, did not stop father from digging a

hole there; after all, his goal was not to get out but

to get further in. The first time my father told me

this story, I jumped ahead as you probably wish to:

what good is it to dig a way inside the barrack? She

cannot escape and even if it was possible, her unique

situation would have alerted the guards soon after.

But father's thoughts were not about *escaping* but

about *comforting*. He tells me that sometimes, there

is truly no exit, but that it is not reason enough to

give up, that it is not worth going forward if the

ground you are currently standing on is completely

rotten.

He dug during the nights for several days,

even until early mornings when he realized how

rarely people came this way. He camouflaged his

tunnel with discarded wooden planks and none were

the wiser. The daily rations given by the enemy were

scarce but enough for my father and so days passed.

Then came the day when my father's fears

materialized. It is true that this barrack had been

hastily constructed, but sadly, they had taken

enough time to put crude yet resistant wooden

boards to act as a floor, but his heart beat evermore.

Through cracks in the floor he could see her: a

woman kneeling, her garments dusty and grey, her

faint chestnut hair dirty and filthy; her eyes, her

bright blue eyes however, pierced the darkness. She

eventually glanced down and saw him before he had

time to utter a single word. The ensuing clanking

sound of her shackles as she approached as far as

she could, portrayed her eagerness.

   "Don't ever leave me again!" she pleaded,

pouring her heart into every syllable.

He fulfilled this request like no one could have ever

done. When morning came, he did not come out of

his tunnel.

Thus began a most *peculiar* relationship.

My mother lived day and night alone in a

barrack; it seems the enemy was not ready to

populate the place just yet; my father lived his life in

a tunnel peering upward. At first, she shared what

little rations she had by squeezing it through the

floor board but as days passed, they had chiselled a

bit of the floor to share more. How hard a life for

both of them... but father said once again that it is

through darkness that a ray of light feels ever so

warm. That day came when they broke the floor

board but only enough for the size of a hand.

"Imagine this moment," my father tells me,

"my eyes gazing into hers, my hand reaching

upward toward the light, hers going down in

I do imagine it.

It is a source of comfort; it is my image of unity, of perfect harmony. When I am alone, when I am scared or when I am doubtful, I remember this hand grasping out of the ground to reach the pleading hand of my shackled mother and I then know that I am never alone; that wherever I am, there is an open hand reaching for me, waiting for

me to hold it.

"We still had to escape captivity, to live in a

world with little future, but all was good for

we had each other."

They will not tell me how long they lived there;

holding hands, being the only thing to look forward

to.

"We thought we were going deaf," father

suddenly said to me.

I tilted my head quizzically and he laughed. It

seems one day, mother felt greatly distraught. Many

grenades and other explosives were eerily dancing in

a devilish choreography in the sky. Panicking, she

inquired to the guard perched at her door who

nearly dismissed her as crazy. He lowered his right

eyebrow and told her that this had been going on for

days. Mother burst out laughing and that granted

her a stiff hit from the butt of a rifle. In fact, mother

was not laughing as a sign of rebellion but because

this is where she realized that she was thoroughly

feeling my father's presence. If together, the two

could silence days of vigorous assault, how bigger of

a sign did they need to acknowledge they were

meant to be together.

Ignoring a war does not make it disappear.

As mother started to pay more attention to the outside world, she was soon realizing that whoever was attacking was also currently winning. The question to ask, in this current day and age, is whether this imminent liberation hides a bigger tyrant or a savior truly. A common enemy was not enough anymore to tighten bonds and form bands of brothers; I say that myself not because I know so, but because these were my father's words as mother kept updating him about the above ground conflict. If they stayed here, they would die; if they escaped, they would *likely* die… a bit of an awkward children

book isn't it? Must I say I have heard every facets of

the word "die", more than what a child my age

should have?

Death should be the sign of the end of a journey, not

the nature of its beginning.

The chaos that reigned around could not

contain the prisoners who were held against their

will; they saw opportunities arise, they fled in all

directions. It is unfathomable to think they all miraculously arrived to the location they wished to flee to, but it is such a nicer world if I make myself believe so. They all ran, yet my mother still had her unique shackle. It was time for father to brave the harsh light once more. He went back the way he came and stood outside. He tells me it was strange to see *new* destruction piled above the *old* destruction. If we are that quick to build and destroy, how many more stories does the ground contain? How many unsung generations lay a few layers underneath this new ground? Bent on adding

destruction of his own, father vigorously tore the

remnants of the door that led to my mother.

"I will build a door that will stand against

everything."

Incidentally, it was the very first time that my

parents stood face to face. Their image had changed

from a hand reaching above ground to the pseudo-heroic silhouette of my shabby father standing by

the door leading to a world of ruins.

"*Where will we go?*" Mother immediately

asked.

I guess one foregoes formalities when war has

erupted around you. Father ripped the chain from

the wall. The chains holding her hand opened, but

part of the shackle on her ankle stayed attached,

probably interested in an adventure of its own. To

help her get up, father took mother by her arm, only

to figure out her worst kept secret: just as I am about

to do right now, mother was and still is... very, very

light. I bet that even when she carried me, together,

we were still lighter than anything father had ever

lifted, and lifted, he did.   Through a swift and

unexpected move, father swung mother's arm

around his neck and grabbed her other arm so that

he could carry her on his back. Leaning her cheek on

his shoulder, she looked at the right side of father's

face and smiled. She told him she could very well

walk, but apparently father did not reply. It was one of those rare times where he was out of words.

Holding mother tightly, he ran outside. Yes, for those wondering, it is perfectly considerable to run while carrying my mother on your back. They ran up a mountain path until the camp they escaped from could scarcely be seen below. They gave a last glance at the land, the camp and the barrack that had inadvertently brought them together. They waved it goodbyes as if it was a close friend that they would never meet again.

"Our second home will have to be just like

that."

Never climb to the top of a mountain if you

are not ready to look at what *it* will show you. There

came a time when father was finally exhausted; yet,

like a stubborn mule, he still held mother tightly. She

kicked his leg, but it would not do; she dealt him a

sharp knee on his behind to finally make him realize

that it was time to stop. He knelt and let her touch

ground for the first time in a long while. As soon as she did so, she raced for the few feet left to the top of the mountain. Father, unable to keep up, says he remembers the moment very well; a moment that pains him up to this day. Mother reached the top first and did not turn around to gloat over her victory; she became as rigid as a stone tablet. She crouched and bawled like a little baby. Father did not rush; he knew exactly why. He walked and stopped beside her, crouched and stared at her face and forced himself not to look forward.

"What did you see?" he nonetheless asked.

"I saw what has become," she stuttered.

"No," she continued.

"No?" he asked.

"It is what I could not see; the world that will

be."

He hugged her; he embraced her, so that she could

believe in the world that will be.

When father woke up the next day, he

initially panicked as he could not see mother on his

side. All was premature when he perceived her

silhouette sitting on a rock. He walked toward her,

to the top of the mountain and silently sat beside

her. They both looked; the panoramic view

presented a destroyed, butchered world.

Regardless, they gazed at its grandeur.

"I can see it," she smiled.

"What do you see?" asked father, reminiscent

of yesterday.

"The world that will be."

She jumped up, her heart racing like it never did

before, her eyes sparkling like the ones of a new

child, perusing the wonders before her; the wonders

you and I would fail to see.

"But, not yet!" she continued, her face frozen

between a smile and a thought.

They carefully walked down the path of the mountain, holding hands. Something did not feel right; not for mother, but definitely for father. As a bird that frantically moves its head around, he looked left, then right and in a quick, sweeping move, he swung mother around him and carried her on his back, just as he did the day before. She chuckled; she described it as a proximity that made them one flesh.

"I can walk," she mentioned.

"I know you can," he replied.

"You don't need to carry me," she continued.

Father stopped and turned his head back to look at her face as best as he humanly could, *"I know you can walk, but wouldn't you rather soar?"* He looked forward once more, *"See,"* he paused, *"you're the one carrying me."*

They needed food and they needed shelter...

as did every other survivor out there. Neither of them were really fit to fend for themselves through any shape of violence and this weighted greatly on father's heart. While father feared the eventuality of meeting hostile men, mother contemplated a scenario of *unity through misery.* He frowned; she smiled. A shiver went through his body; a shiver went through hers.

"I can hear the waves of the ocean..." she

softly murmured.

*"The water must be tainted, the gusting wind

transporting its diseases..."* father murmured

back.

Mother tilted her head; her inquisitive eyes strong

enough to make father stop.

"Who is this man I am talking to? 'tis the

man of whom I sought counsel; who brought

me liberation? Bring him back won't you?"

"I need you so..." is the only statement father

made under his breath.

He says that, since then, he clung to her ever harder.

There were no madmen, no wolves in sheep's

clothing; if they did exist, they lived in a world far

more prosperous or dangerous than the one my

parents had stumbled upon. Through their travels,

they did cross path with survivors but only to

exchange directions, barter supplies and share an

odd story or two. Never did they fear for their own

safety; peace, peace at last.

       They picked a house on the beach whose

walls could be repaired and ceiling fixed. They

buried the previous owners and adopted the place as

their own.

This is when the world we lived in became the world

that will be.

PART 2 – THE WORLD THAT WILL BE

My mother was lying down

The bomb was in the sky

She was in lovely agony

They were witnessing misery

Her pain would be bringing joy

Their tears would be heard no more

Through their naked eyes they saw

the light, the new destroyer

I cried for the first time.

The world cried no more.

As I was given birth, countless had lost their lives and yet mine, had just started. My parents were spared but the land had bled once too many time; they would have to move. My father could not carry my mother like he used to for I was now in the way. In his words, it also meant that she could not

carry him as well. Through the material they had

gathered, I was fashioned a pouch that my mother

could wear as a backpack. The unforeseen

consequence of this pouch was that I was forced to

look *backward.* Nothing ever came toward me; I was

forced to stare at the shrinking locations that we

would visit no more; I would see houses getting

smaller, lands disappearing and friendly faces fading.

Through my eyes, nothing was created; everything I

saw was meant to disappear. My father tells me

that, in a way, those memories of mine hold the

truth; they are here in me to prove that my life was

not to start in a destroyed world, but that I would

exist on something new, on something never seen by

anyone.

In the countless days that ensued; I rarely felt

loved, for my parents did not have time for me.

What were they fleeing from? I did not know.

Where were they fleeing to? They knew not either.

In truth, we would only stop when either father or

mother would collapse from exhaustion, and even

then, our stay was very short.

I was not even a year old when it came time

for my first solo adventure, much to the chagrin of

my parents. When I echo my regrets from the

actions of my younger self, father pleasantly repeats

the same words of wisdom: *"It's not your fault that

you're the most amazing girl ever!"*

I got to say, he is pretty good at cheering me up!

It all started with a butterfly, a single butterfly

too eager to go wherever free butterflies wish to go.

Mother was holding me in her arms when she

spotted a butterfly fluttering a few feet in front of us;

she says I spotted it first, but for some reason, I

doubt it. Surely feeling the gaze of our burning eyes

on its wings, the butterfly decided to dart past us. It

brushed on my mother's right cheek. I swatted for it

but missed. Mother jerked her head back to see

where the butterfly was going but in doing so, lost

footing, slipped and fell. I landed dazed on mother's

stomach when we collectively realized that our new

ordeal was far from over. As a mouth who playfully

slurps the last noodle in a big bowl of soup, the earth

sucked us in; we only fell a few feet beneath, but

enough to separate us from father. The earth had

closed itself in a way that allowed father to witness

this newfound horror through a tiny hole made of a

mixture of soil, rocks and debris. Mother shouldered

all of the impact for me, she stayed on her back and I

fell on her side. Seemingly continuing its divine

comedy, the earth pulled the same trick once more.

The ground shook and this time, I was the only one

to be swallowed whole. This time, the fall had been

more than a mere couple of feet.

"Darling, she's dead! Oh God, she's dead!"

still echoes in my head to this day.

Of course, I was not. Can the dead write? Can they?

My father downplays and light-heartedly recollects this era as the time in which we suddenly became the owners of an apartment complex, but in reality, he must have been mortified. Through a hole in the ground, he could see mother laying on her back as well as another hole where he could see me laying on dirt far below.

"She's alive!" he said.

I am alive.

Believe it or not, this remarkable situation

persisted and went on for a few days. If you do not

know much about diapers, it is best for you to figure

that out at this moment. Father, our family's only

ground dweller would scavenge for food and liquid,

would lower it down to my mother who would take

her share and send it down to me. They would then

wait in anticipation to see if I would be smart enough

to eat the food and drink the liquid. I was slow, but

it turns out that I was smart enough. Sadly, I was not

smart enough to reattach any container they gave me to haul it back up to the surface and as such, father would always have to find more and more containers. On the positive side, I was building myself quite the impressive fort.

Father would use the remainder of his strength to dig his way to mother but it was not easy, as if the earth had completely forgot that it had once caved in. Mother, who vividly insisted that she had no broken bones, still laid on her back with her broken bones; the situation was making her nervous

for you see, although she could see father, she could

not look at me. Eventually, father's effort became

apparent. With a wider hole came easier provisions

transportation as well as the giddy anticipation that

he would one day be able to slip through it. But with

it came, as you might have already guessed,

something far more precious, far more symbolic for

them. Lying on his stomach, father extended his arm

as far as he humanly could, possibly even beyond

that; it gave mother enough strength to shriek past

the pain, sit and extend her arm to the sky.

They held hands once again.

The beach house...

The atomic bombs...

The detainment camp...

The cell...

Darkness...

hands...

It all flashed in front of their eyes and, as if

given a new life, mother was able to get up. *"Look..."*

father said in a serene voice pointing at me, a tone of

voice that would soon change. Mother looked at his

peaceful eyes and turned her head around to look at

me.

I took my first step

I took my second step

I looked up and giggled

My parents were proud

I took a fifth step

I took a sixth step

They could see me no more

My parents were horrified

It seems I chose quite the wrong time to learn

how to walk. Father jumped down to mother's level

and jumped down to mine. When I asked how he did

so, he replied: *"For you my daughter, I have ripped rocks in half."* I always reply *"Yikes!"* It seems like the only reply worth giving.

As small and inexperienced as I was, I was still long gone when father reached my level.

The tunnel was deep and dark; its only possible point of interest came from the cackling sound of a distant fire, which also acted as its only source of light.

Mother held father's arm tightly, shouting my name,

profusely indifferent of whom or what she might

wake up by yelling like that. Slowly but surely, they

moved onward.

crick

crack

crunch

As each new step was taken, the mystery

remained: how could I walk this far without hurting

myself? My parents were proud of this brand-new

ability of mine, but probably hoped that I had chosen

a different time to practice it. They finally arrived at

the fire to discover... a very dirty sooth-filled me

sleeping by the fire.

"She's sleeping?" he said in great confusion.

"She's sleeping," she sighed with great relief.

As great as the fire had been, it had to be put

out in order to escape and reach the outside world

once more. Only through the light of day, could my

parents stare at each other and openly laugh about

how dirty we all were, but alas, water was not a commodity. Rivers, contaminated as they were, had become a fact of life, but even those were nowhere to be seen. Our last resort was to use boiled water… but it still required water… and something to boil it with. Yeah, we were in a pickle, a very dusty, dirty pickle.

We walked for three more days; well actually mother and father walked; mother insisted in carrying me regardless of my newly found, yet badly-timed ability.   We did not cross encampments,

houses or remnants of old villages; father's

provisions were getting low. Regardless, from that

day he came to our rescue, he never stopped smiling.

In a destroyed world, with no other human contacts

than our own family, he was *content*.

How many days passed?

Against all expectations, like a mirage that only appears when all hope is lost, we came face-to-face to a new world: the mansion of many doors.

I do not expect you to understand the mansion of many doors but frankly I have used a lot of fancy words in this story and in the days where you understand my words I pray that you understand that this mansion really existed for us.

PART 3 – THE MANSION OF MANY DOORS

A mansion... Standing its ground like a fierce,

impressive beast, high and mighty, resisting,

unimpressed, the fate of the world. From where we

were standing, its main entrance and two visible

wings made us think that it was in a *U-shape* but we

would soon find out upon entering that three more

wings existed. In the end, the mansion is shaped like

a crude hand-drawn star, a star that shone brightly; a

star that was shining just for us. Although it had

definitely felt the ravage of war, the mansion of

many doors still had its walls, ceiling and a good

amount of windows, a stark contrast to its

immediate surroundings.

"How can it stand amidst the rubbles?"

Mother asked.

"Houses made of dust will return to dust,

houses built on sand will collapse..." Father

started until I kicked the allegories out of him,

"it's... a house made to resist."

Running rather than walking and barging

rather than opening, we entered the connecting

main building. In it stood very little aside from an

excess of dust and a small table where a flickering

lamp stood. I could not grasp what was awe-worthy,

but my parents precipitated themselves,

understandably not sharing the same feeling. They

stood in front of the lamp, both hands firmly pressed

on the table. They stared as if they had been

hypnotized.

Reflecting on the matter, is it not sweet that this gigantic, empty space had suddenly brought more hope to my parents than if it had been a luxurious, furnished entrance with towering statues and chandeliers? A lamp, a flickering lamp was all it had, all they ever needed.

In its present state, all the other wings were closed off by doors of various sizes. Father started his attempt at opening doors starting from the left, while mother attempted her best from the right. I stood in the center of the room, trying to guess which one would be the lucky one. My guess was initially incorrect because they both reunited back near me without a single door open. Mother suggested that we go back outside and see if there is another entrance we can try, while father was advocating a more violent and destructive approach while I, I silently protested that they had been too

tired to try the only door that was obviously not even

closed and left ajar.

I raised my finger and pointed at it and was soon

deemed a hero.

"*Didn't we try that door?*" inquired father.

"*Did we see that door?*" replied mother.

"*Maybe we didn't look for it.*"

Father placed me back on the ground and pushed me

forward.

"It's your door, you open it."

Father says that unlike in castles found in

fairy tales, the massive door was actually really hard

for a child to budge. I pushed mighty hard, as if I was

the only one that could truly open this door and with

my parents brilliantly looking at their exhausted

daughter, I finally completed my task. With the door

out of the way, we could all gaze at a remarkably

long and pristine corridor that led to what we could

only call the *White Room*.

The corridor leading to the *White Room* was

so clean and unspoiled that mother felt ashamed

about how dirty we all were. She asked father to

refrain from touching the walls and immediately took

me in her arms. Father laughed, but did not argue,

without saying a word, he walked to the archway of

the *White Room*. Still in the distance, that room was

shining like a big neon light. We would definitely get

that place dirty!

"I don't like walking toward the light..." father

sighed, *"well, not yet, anyway."*

The *White Room* was white.

The *White Room* was clean.

The *White Room* was made to

make us clean.

To say that the *White Room* was a bathroom would

be to say that this mansion was a cottage. The *White*

Room did not have any other door. It had more than

several sinks attached to its walls, but aside from

that, it had nothing more than a giant swimming pool

filled with surprisingly clean water. I waved my arms

and legs wildly in excitement, trying to escape the

clutches of my mother but she kept fighting back.

Father gave a puzzled look at my mother and he too

waved his arms and legs as I just did.

"Look at how clean the water is," she said,

definitely troubled.

"Clean water serves no purpose if it is to

remain clean."

"I know... but,"

"And besides, there's no other door here, no

place to get clean beforehand."

"I know... but,"

"Alright, let's think hard and clear about this."

He brought his hands to his waist and made himself

look like he was in deep thoughts something which

even at my age sounded and screamed like a huge

diversion. As expected, his next move was to use his

well-positioned hands to remove his clothes and run

to the pool while chanting *"mwahaha!"* He jumped

in the pool; mother felt tricked. I giggled; mother

sighed and let me go. In a matter of seconds, I had

mimicked father all down to his evil laughter:

"mwheeheehee." He lifted and placed me on the

low-end where I could stand up on the tip of my

toes. He flipped around and rested on the edge, staring at mother until her will broke and she decided to join us.

Plenty of subjects were discussed during bath time such as mother's preoccupation that we should have looked for the owner before jumping in; we also touched on father's current complete lack of preoccupations. They both agreed on how this speck of time was such a sudden, appreciated moment of respite and even if it may not last, it was surely well treasured. For now, we were escaping the outside

world; a world filled with bombs, deaths and

diseases, a world we currently did not know.

This mansion has many doors and even after all

those years, the *White Room* was still among my

favourite, because it treated us with something we

did not deserve. Every time I would fall down and

get a bruise, a visit to the *White Room* would wash it

all away, body and mind.

Satisfied with our current state of cleanliness and having passed mother's sanitation scrutiny, we marched back to the connecting building. After all, even though one wing led to the *White Room*, there were still four more to discover. The first issue we discovered was that the main entrance door had violently been dancing in the wind and new dusty dunes were starting to reclaim this place. Father rushed to the door. Before closing it, he suddenly paused, long enough for mother to inquire. Through a quick manoeuvre he retrieved the key from the main entrance door. Yes, a key left in a keyhole, as

simple as that. We had rushed inside eager to see

what it had to offer, yet we had not even took the

time to check the door better; can you think what

would have happened if the wind had dislodged the

key somehow? It was a single key though and

mother did voice the concern that it was unlikely

going to open all the doors here. Father reassured

her, saying that those who resisted would meet *"my*

foot." He then made the motion of kicking a door so

vividly that he says I was disappointed when mother

shrugged it off as a last resort.

We all held hands as a big family as we stood

in front of the leftmost door. He says this moment

brings back good memories, because it was more

than just unlocking a physical door. He placed the

key in the keyhole, turned the handle and pushed

the door open. It revealed a corridor with more

other doors.

To fast forward a little bit through our door-

opening antics, there were two wings like the current

one; they both involved rather plain corridors with

bedrooms. Yes, lots of bedrooms. These were

rooms of various size, each holding various furniture.

They were well kept, but none showed any recent

activity.

Being hungry, and knowing that this place

could not be made of bedrooms and a bath alone,

we were once again unlocking the door to a new

aisle.

Father gave me the key, telling me that I had a knack

for discovering cool stuff. From the center of the

room, I started to wobble to a door we had already

unlocked. Father said *"stupid baby,"* and spun me to

a direction of a locked door. Mother gave him the

evil eyes for having jokingly called me stupid, but he

in returns gave her sad eyes. This time, I picked the

right door and worked for a few minutes trying to get

the key to fit in that hole like I had seen it done

before.   After some arduous coaching from my

parents, I finally pushed the door open.

It is as this moment that my parents were

painfully reminded that they existed in the real world

and not a pure fantasy, that even though this

mansion was a pure blessing, that they would still

have to work hard. The mansion was a gift, but life

still goes on.

"That's odd," mother categorized as she

witnessed it all.

You see, in all fairness there was nothing truly

odd in this dining area; it is in its contrast that it

became abnormal. It had a modest-sized, dust-laden

table with a few chairs made to roughly

accommodate a dozen people; in the back was a

kitchen area. There lied a great deal of silverware

utensils and other cooking instruments. Some were

on the ground, some were shattered and the rest

were dirty. Cobwebs and all, the room looked like a

traditional post-apocalyptic dining area. When you

consider that this room existed in the same mansion

as the *White Room*, one has to wonder what it all

means.

Fantasy lived right next to reality.

In the years to come, the *White Room*

became a *Chamber of Respite* where we could relax

while the dining area became a *Chamber of Strength*

were we held each other. I think... I think everyone,

even you, have these two rooms whether you realize

it or not.

Don't you? Do you have a *Chamber of Respite* that

contrasts to your *Chamber of Strength?*

        As hungry as we were, we had to tidy up as

the room was strongly pleading for a good tidying.

While throwing away spoiled food, mother found a

great deal of canned food, delicacy of this modern

age. We blessed the food, for truly, we were blessed

and ate. Too small to sit on my own chair, I sat on

mother's laps, wondering if I would see the day

where I occupied my own chair.

Let us continue that story but stay in that room.

Let us come back to that same room, at the same

time of the day... but a few years later.

My father sat in front of me and my mother

stood on my right, I blew on the candles that proudly

stood on a portion of spam. It was my favourite dish,

still is.

I was now six years old.

I was standing on my very own chair, grinning

enthusiastically as my father and mother clapped.

As they continued clapping, my mind kept

racing through my memories.

I remembered the innocent joy I had every

time I decided to switch bedrooms. I would move all

the belongings I had and felt like I had a new

universe to explore.

I remembered every other day when father

would leave home to scout for provisions and

survivors. At first, I would have to say I was selfishly

happy that father never brought anyone back home.

I would sometimes dream that he did so; he would

bring home a lone traveller, a couple or an entire

family and instead of being happy, I felt like my

parents would not treat me as family anymore. I

know they would never do that, so now I feel pain in

my stomach when father comes back home, saying

that no one needed shelter.

In truth, I think he softens it up for me. I bet he does

not even *find* survivors.

I remembered the days when mother creatively cooked our dishes or knit us new clothes. It is obvious that I tore my fair share of fabrics but mother always replied saying that she was very grateful that I inherited her genes in regards to how little growing up I actually did.

I remembered the days when my parents would decide to change roles. Father would be the one to stay and cook, clean and tickle me silly while mother would be the one to venture out. Although

father was in no way strong or muscular, when

compared to mother, he was a titan. So, I asked him

once, if he was scared that mother would be the one

to go out.

He replied, *"but when daddy leaves, it is

mommy that is terrified."*

They stopped clapping and I clapped a little bit on my

own.

For the past few years, my birthday present had

been quite special and unique. It is something that

you would probably find silly, childish and awkward.

On my birthday, father would break one of the doors

that he had grammatically called the *unbargeable*

doors. You see, after all these years, we had

unlocked everything that could be unlocked. Some

cooperated through the twist of a key while others

responded more gracefully to father's foot or elbow.

However, a few reinforced doors mocked all of that

and systematically required more effort and destruction. It was then bizarrely and suddenly decided that these doors would be opened when the *time was right*. It also allowed the mansion to retain a flair of mystery. I know what you might be thinking though,

> *"Hey! If the world you live in is so harsh,*
>
> *shouldn't you take all that is given to you?*
>
> *What lies behind those doors might make*
>
> *your life easier, happier, better!"*

On the first point, you may be correct: three months

after we arrived, one of the *unbargeable doors*

revealed a delicate set of threads and needles that

definitely made our clothes last longer. However,

father's decision was to tell me and tell you in return

that we *could not* be happier and better if we were

already happy to begin with. Being happy is not

about what you can have; it's about what is already

around you and it's not like we could actually easily

break those doors. Some were in metal; some

require blowtorches and fluids to make all those

instruments work! I am pretty sure that father

always opened those doors as soon as he had

everything he needed to do so. This is not to say

that I was not curious; it sure had become a fun

birthday tradition.

Father nodded and I jumped off my chair.

Oh, I already knew which door to pick this year. On a

windy day, I happened to walk by a door where I

could hear the faint rustling of the wind. It felt far

away, high above me; I knew that it wasn't any room,

it was *the* room. I ran as fast as I could and my

parents followed behind. He swooped mother and

put her on his back like *"the good old days when the*

world had just died." A few turns later, I stopped.

He kneeled to let mother down and looked rather

proud when he saw the door I had picked.

He readied his shoulder for a tackle.

"We need that shoulder, darling,"

refused mother.

He brought his right leg up, so much so that

he nearly hit his chin with his knee.

"We also need your foot, dear."

He spun around and leaned forward, butt-first

toward the door. He grinned at Mother, which

awarded him the evil eyes for not daring to continue

this charade.

He got up, turned around and pushed the door with

the palm of his hand; it opened. I looked up at him

in astonishment as if he had performed a death-

defying magic trick. Wrapping my head around it, I

finally realized that father must have known the

whole time what I was thinking about.

"Oh, dad..." I blurted, holding up my tears as

best as I could.

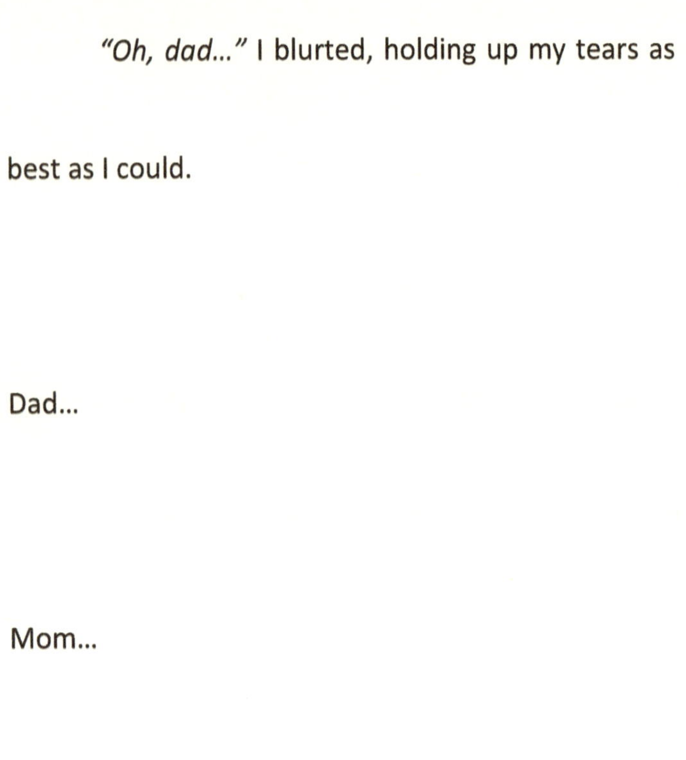

Dad...

Mom...

Mother embraced me and I cried my heart out. Yes,

can you imagine it? My birthday cake was a portion

of spam with a candle and my gift was an unlocked

door. Yet, I was happy, so happy.

After a teary session, I finally got into my

newly discovered room to find out that it was not

really a door at all, but more of a narrow spiral

staircase.

"*Oh!*" went mother.

"*Wondered when you'd get to it,*" went

father.

I had only recently noticed that the mansion seemed to have a lookout tower and upon realizing that, I tried to guess behind which door it hid. Its secret was revealed on that windy day. As I walked up the stairs, I felt a bit puzzled; after all, the lookout tower could have provided a very good view for father to find survivors. Why had he not searched for it earlier?

Step by step, we climbed, enough to get dizzy doing it. At the top was a very small room with nothing more than a wooden chair and three windows that gave a very good panoramic view. I asked that it became my new bedroom, but my parents refused. In the end, we compromised and it became one of my many playrooms.

In the upcoming days, father helped me bring the bigger toys like my rocking horse all the way up there. My newfound joy here was to be on my horse while spotting either of my parents coming back in the distance. I would normally have enough time to run downstairs and greet them at the front entrance.

From up there, I could now see *everything*; I wonder

if that was entirely a good thing. With that thought, I

started to wonder if the last person to have been in

the lookout tower shared the same feeling.

I found an answer to my question not long

afterward.

One day, I was sitting on the floor, drawing a

colony of snakes I had seen, these guys had inherited

the earth... then the ground shook heavily.   No

sooner than that was finished that I heard my

mother asking if I was all right. I replied that I was

fine but my eye got distracted.

A brick on the wall had come loose.

Taking all the credit for this discovery, I opened my

eyes wide in anticipation of what I had unearthed. If

the doors held gigantic secrets what were the secrets

hidden behind the walls.

I removed the brick and looked in that secret cache it

revealed; I had found a scrapbook.   Quickly, I

snatched it away, as if it was a matter of time before

it disappeared.

It held no great work of art but art nonetheless.

The first image depicted a man sitting at a

desk in an office. All the surrounding white walls are

nearly crushing him. The man is either angry or

impatient; he is staring at his watch. Although his

desk is riddled with papers and objects, it does not

seem to be messy because of the war. It seems to be

before all of that.

The second image is somewhat similar to the

first. The man is still sitting down, but the walls have

fallen. His desk is overturned and his watch is

noticeably broken. His mouth, only a single

horizontal stroke, depicts a man that is neither angry

nor happy. At least he is not angry anymore.

The third image is completely dark. Written

in white, sounds of people yelling and crying litter

the space; it is either night-time or maybe he has his

eyes closed? A portion of the image is not dark; here

we see a woman in rags. I can only see a dirty face

and a bit of her neck.

I continue flipping through the book as the

story becomes more and more familiar. One of them

has a house on the beach. The sun is shining and the

house looks remarkable. So much so, that I wonder

if this image was drawn before or after the war.

Mother calls me for dinner and I flip through

the rest. As I peer at the last image, I look around

the room with a big smile on my face. I feel happy; I

feel a connection. The image depicts a young girl,

next to a rocking horse in the lookout tower, going

through the scrapbook.

Mother calls me for a second time. Instead of hiding

the scrapbook, I decide to conceal it my pocket and I

rush downstairs.

     We are all sitting at the dinner table. Father

looks relatively tense. My mind races between the

thoughts of my discovery and the thoughts of what

he is going through.

     "They threw a volley south of here," he finally

said.

While I stay silent, mother gets up and

massages his back. I do not understand it myself, not

the back massage, but the volley of bombs. What is

there to destroy? What is there to conquer? I am

both filled with rage and curiosity as I anticipate that

we will have to move. Father is still looking confused

and in an attempt to cheer him up, I am about to pull

the scrapbook when mother reacts first. *"Let's just*

take a bath," she proposes. He mumbles but I react

cheerfully in his stead. I walk under the table to get

to his side and pull on his arm; he concedes.

We are in the low-end. Father and mother

are sitting, their back firmly resting. I still have to

stand as sitting means water in my nostrils and even

if I could, I rarely want to stand still anyway. Being a

bit too silent for my liking, I remember the scrapbook

and I know that it will cheer him up. I tell them to

wait and I leave to go get the notebook. I get back in

carefully so to not drop it in the water. I make my

way up to mother and father and I lean on his right

arm. He turns his head and notices the book. He

forcibly smiles,

"So, you've finally found it," he says, *"it took*

you nearly a whole year."

We went through most images together;

father and mother would alternate as they told the

story behind each image. It normally ended with one

teasing the other and one getting a terrible watery

splashy wave of judgement. When we finally arrived

to the final image where I am shown in the lookout

tower reading the scrapbook, father simply tells me

that he knew that one day, his secret hideout would

become mine. As I closed the book, the earth shook

once more, enough for me to lose my grip and

witness in horror as the book fell in the water. I

gasped and immediately plunged my arm in the

water so to retrieve it, but father catches my wrist

first. He brings our hands above the water, right

beside my mouth, right beside his. We look down at

the book, as the images slowly fade away.

      "Let the images wash away, but keep the

memories."

      By the time we left the *White Room*, night

had truly fallen and again, the ground shook.

Mother and Father opened the entrance door while I

decided to steal a glance from my tower.

My rocking horse fell on its side

    My tea table was vaporized

My dolls crumbled and fell as well

    My swing set ripped in twain

My boyish dusty hair danced in the wind

    My ever blue eyes stared at the sky

My tower was split in half

    My feet were in the air

For the first time, I clenched the sky

    For the last time, the tower died

I flew high in my tower

My tower high in the sky

...but my tower brought me down.

The past was gone; the future was looking to be a

concern once more but the present... The present is

where I must live in. No, don't read this believing I

have died! My story is not over!

crick

crack

The sound of a new life!

splich

spluch

No, of an old life worth insisting!

ping

pang

Of a life worth pursuing!

tak

tok

A light in the distance!

clunk

clank

No, a light close by!

I am Sabbath

...

I am Sabbath

...

I am Sabbath, I am seven, I am rest, and I am the

extra breath of life needed for a journey where we

can travel no further.

I am Sabbath and my journey is not over; my purpose

is not fulfilled. Through it, Death cannot touch me.

> *I lift my right arm*

> *It is bruised, it is weary*

> *I look at the back, the palm of my hand*

> *Yes, it is still my hand*

> *I plunge it forward*

> *Into the light*

> *In the light is my father's hand*

The reaching hand I take

It is the same hand I have heard in the stories

This hand is just for me

I get it now; this hand is just for me.

I simply need to reach for it.